Why Is He Spreading Rumors About Me?

TEACHER AND COUNSELOR ACTIVITY GUIDE

Boys Town, Nebraska

by Jennifer Licate   Illustrated by Suzanne Beaky

Why Is He Spreading Rumors about Me?
Text and Illustrations Copyright © 2022 by Father Flanagan's Boys' Home
ISBN: 978-0-938510-69-7

Published by the Boys Town Press
13603 Flanagan Blvd.
Boys Town, NE 68010

All rights reserved under International and Pan-American Copyright Conventions. Unless otherwise noted, no part of this book may be reproduced, stored in a retrieval system, or transmitted in any form or by any means, electronic, mechanical, photocopying, recording or otherwise, without express written permission of the publisher, except for brief quotations or critical reviews.

For a Boys Town Press catalog, call **1-800-282-6657**
or visit our website: **BoysTownPress.org**

All Discussion Questions, Worksheets, and Activities are available for download.

ACCESS:
https://www.boystownpress.org/book-downloads

ENTER:
Your first and last names
Email address
Code: 938510wsrmag697
Check "yes" to receive emails to ensure your email link is received.

Printed in the United States
10 9 8 7 6 5 4 3 2

Boys Town Press is the publishing division of Boys Town, a national organization serving children and families.

Table of Contents

Chapter 1
Story..5
Discussion Questions......................................8
Activities..11

Chapter 2
Story..15
Discussion Questions....................................18
Activities...20

Chapter 3
Story..23
Discussion Questions....................................26
Activities...28

Chapter 4
Story..33
Discussion Questions....................................36
Activities...38

Chapter 5
Story... 41
Discussion Questions.................................... 45
Activities... 47

Chapter 6
Story..51
Discussion Questions....................................56
Activities...58

TEACHER AND COUNSELOR ACTIVITY GUIDE

Chapter 1

I'm Mateo. I'm a happy kid who tries to see the best in every situation. Heck, I even like going to school. You may think that's weird, but I'm the guy who gets excited when it's time to go back to school after long breaks. Of course, I don't admit that to my buddies. They'd probably laugh and not believe me anyway. My parents tell everyone I love school. I think they're right.

Classes and studying aren't why I like school. It's more about being around my friends and joking around with them. My good buddies are Tyler and Malik. We've been pals for years.

IF I WASN'T AT SCHOOL, I'D BE STUCK AT HOME. I don't do a lot of after-school activities because my parents need help looking after my siblings. I have three younger brothers and a younger sister, and each one is a handful. My parents depend on me – the free babysitter – to help out as much as I can. I don't mind. It's fun, mostly, but definitely **EXHAUSTING.** Being in school gives me a break, which is a funny way to think about school.

So far, the school year's been good and bad. Sometimes teachers get on my case about incomplete homework, but they're mostly cool about it. **I THINK THEY KNOW I TRY HARD EVEN THOUGH I HAVE A LOT OF RESPONSIBILITIES AT HOME.**

Lunch, obviously, is the best part of my school day. I get to hang out with Tyler, Malik, and my other friends. But today it wasn't fun, and I blame Harris.

The trouble started when Lily walked over and talked to me. She's the only friend I have who's a girl. I don't have a lot in common with most girls, but Lily and I've known each other since we were little. I like that she doesn't get all weird about little things. There's no drama with her. She's really funny, too. She did a laugh-out-loud imitation of her mom yelling about how Lily needs to clean her room. Her mom's nice but is super strict about keeping the house clean. Anyway, the guys noticed Lily and I laughing. They stared at us, and then Harris started in with me.

"Do you have a new girlfriend, Mateo?" he snickered.

"Yeah, she's my girl... friend," I joked. To make sure everyone knew I was just goofing, I used my fingers to make air quotes when I said it.

Lily called him out, too. She rolled her eyes and, with lots of snark, said, "SERIOUSLY, HARRIS?"

"Well, it looked like you two were on a date over there," swore Harris.

Then the bell rang. Lunch was over. We all grabbed our books and left the cafeteria. As I walked to class, I thought about what Harris had said. **I USUALLY GET ALONG WITH HIM, BUT BOY DOES HE LIKE TO STIR STUFF UP. HE LOOKS FOR DRAMA WHERE THERE ISN'T ANY.** I don't know why he had to make a big deal about me and Lily goofing around. It's not like I want her to be my girlfriend. I feel kinda embarrassed just thinking of her that way.

CHAPTER ONE

Follow-Up Discussion Questions and Activities

Discussion Questions

1. Do you ever consider school to be a welcome break from being at home?
   _____
   _____
   _____

   • Why or why not?
      _____
      _____
      _____

2. Mateo's favorite part of the school day is lunch. What do you enjoy most when you're at school?
   _____
   _____
   _____

3. Do you think most kids consider lunch to be the best part of their school day? Why might a student not enjoy the lunch period?
   _____
   _____
   _____

4. Mateo doesn't have many female friends. Are most of your friends the same gender as you, or do you have more opposite-gender friendships? Why do you think that is?
   _____
   _____
   _____

5. When Harris asked Mateo if Lily was his girlfriend, do you think he was teasing or was he being sincere and genuine?

___

- Why do you feel that way?

___

- Have you ever had a friend or classmate ask you a question that made you think they were trying to be mean or embarrass you?

___

6. Mateo responded to Harris by laughing it off. Do you think Mateo handled the situation well?

___

- Why or why not?

___

7. In what other ways could Mateo have responded to Harris?

- Examples can include the following: Mateo yells at Harris to mind his own business; Mateo ignores him; Mateo gets in his face and challenges him to a fight.

8. Do you think Mateo considers Harris a friend?

- Why or why not?

Activities

Creative Writing Activity

1. Provide the following instructions to the class: Earlier, we discussed several reasons why some students dread lunchtime. Imagine you dislike lunchtime because of one of those reasons, or make up your own. Write a short story or draw a comic strip explaining how you would solve the problem or situation.

2. Ask for volunteers to share their stories or comic strips with the class.

Class Discussion Activity

1. Explain to students: Earlier we discussed different ways Mateo could have responded to Harris. (Ask students to recall their answers while you write them on the board).

2. Have each student choose the response they think is best for Mateo, then group students according to the response they chose.

3. Instruct each group to create a list of the possible outcomes of that response.

4. After identifying possible outcomes, ask each group if they still think their response is the best one for Mateo. (Encourage debate. Groups should be prepared to defend their decision.)

Why Is He Spreading Rumors About Me?

CREATIVE WRITING ACTIVITY WORKSHEET

Write a short story or draw a comic strip explaining how you would solve your lunchroom problem or situation.

Short Story:
_____
_____
_____
_____

Comic Strip:

Why Is He Spreading Rumors About Me?

Class Discussion Activity Worksheet

Create a list of the possible outcomes if **Mateo** had responded your way.

Possible Outcomes:
_____
_____
_____
_____
_____
_____
_____

TEACHER AND COUNSELOR ACTIVITY GUIDE

Chapter 2

WHAT HAPPENED AT LUNCH BUGGED ME, BUT THE REST OF THE AFTERNOON WENT OKAY. After last period, I walked to my locker thinking about Harris and what went down in the cafeteria. I was so deep in thought, I didn't even notice my friend Josh.

"Hey, Mateo!" he yelled.

"Oh, what's up dude."

"**I HEARD YOU HAVE A GIRRRLLL-FRIEND!**"

It took me a second to figure out what Josh was talking about.

"You must have heard that from Harris, but he's lying," I said. "Lily IS NOT my girlfriend."

"If you say so, bro," Josh said, sort of mocking me.

MY MIND WAS SPINNING WITH SO MANY QUESTIONS.

Why is Harris lying about me? He doesn't actually think Lily's my girlfriend, does he?
No, he'd know if she was my girlfriend! Maybe he thinks I like her, like I have THOSE kinds of feelings for her? Could be he's trying to get a rise out of me because he's bored or jealous? Who knows, but he shouldn't be making up rumors about me! We're supposed to be friends. Geez! Who's he telling anyway? Josh and who else?

"Mateo! Mateo!"

Now who's yelling my name?

"Mateo! We heard some news about you… that you have a girlfriend," Amir said.

"Wrong! I don't have a girlfriend."

"Well, everyone's been saying you and Lily are crushing on each other," blurted Benjamin.

"WHAT? HARRIS IS JUST SPREADING RUMORS AGAIN. LILY'S A FRIEND! JUST A FRIEND! I DON'T KNOW WHY THIS IS BECOMING SUCH A BIG THING TODAY!"

"Hey, I'm just saying what I heard. Harris even told us you admitted she was, so don't try denying it now," Amir insisted.

"STOP! I was only joking. Harris knows that. He's just making trouble like he always does. I can't believe you'd actually believe him!"

Amir wouldn't drop it. "He told us you two were pretty cozy at lunch."

"If Lily was my girlfriend, I'd admit it. BUT SHE'S NOT!"

Amir put up his hands, as if surrendering, and gave me a half-hearted "sorry." I guess he FINALLY believed me. But then he said something that made me feel sick to my stomach – Harris has been talking about me and Lily all day, and the whole school believes him.

Amir and Benjamin walked off. Their last words to me were "go talk to Harris."

Now I wasn't just annoyed, I was angry and upset. I kept thinking about Harris and the rumor. Why does everyone believe him? Why is this rumor all over school? Everyone's talking about it! Why? So what if Lily and I were really boyfriend and girlfriend, who cares! Lily's cool and all, but I don't like her like that. I don't want everyone thinking we're an item when we're not. It's embarrassing! What's up with Harris?

I thought we were friends. Why would he do this to me?

SOMEHOW, I'VE GOT TO fix THIS.

CHAPTER TWO

Follow-Up Discussion Questions and Activities

Discussion Questions

1. Why do you think Mateo was upset by the rumor about him having a girlfriend?

2. Do you have friends who spread rumors?

3. Could you be friends with someone who spreads rumors about you?

    - Why or why not?

4. Why do you think Harris started the rumor about Mateo and Lily?

5. Do you think Mateo responded appropriately to his friends when they told him they had heard the rumor?

   _____
   _____
   _____

   • Why or why not?

      _____
      _____
      _____

   • How else could Mateo have responded? Examples can include the following: Mateo ignores them; Mateo yells, denies the rumor, and threatens to fight; Mateo shuts them down with a dismissive comment, such as, "I'm not talking about it."

      _____
      _____
      _____

6. Why do you think Mateo is embarrassed by the rumor?

   _____
   _____
   _____

Activities

Class Discussion Activity

1. Ask students: Do you think Mateo reacted the right way when his friends said they had heard the rumor about him and Lily? How would you have reacted in that situation? (Write the responses on the board.)

2. Instruct students to choose the reaction they think is best from the list on the board, then group students according to their choice.

3. Instruct each group to list the possible outcomes of the reaction they selected. After listing several possible outcomes, have them decide if that reaction is still a good choice for Mateo.

4. Instruct each group to share their list of possible outcomes with the class, and whether they still believe it is the best option for Mateo. (Encourage debate. Groups should be prepared to defend their decision.)

Self-Reflection Activity

1. Imagine a rumor is being spread about you. Write a short story (or draw a comic strip or make a list of events) that details the rumor, your response, and the outcome. Encourage students to include the different emotions (embarrassment, shame, anger, confusion, disappointment, relief, happiness, etc.) they experience as they deal with the rumor.
    - Would you feel embarrassed and angry, like Mateo, or would you experience different emotions?

Why Is He Spreading Rumors About Me?

Self-Reflection Activity Worksheet

Imagine a rumor is being spread about you. Write a short story (or list the events that happen) or draw a comic strip that explains how you deal with it. Name what the rumor is and the emotions you experience.

Short Story or List of Events:

_____
_____
_____
_____

Comic Strip:

TEACHER AND COUNSELOR ACTIVITY GUIDE

Chapter 3

When I got home from school, I didn't want to talk to anyone. I just wanted to be by myself. But as soon as I walked through the door, my little brother, Gabriel, ran right at me.

"Mateo! Let's play a game. Come on… PULEEZE!" He pulled hard on my hand and dragged me toward his game. I resisted.

"Not right now, Gabe. Maybe later."

He immediately put on his sad face. I felt guilty that I didn't have time to play, but I needed to be alone. I had to figure out how to shut Harris up and stop the rumor. I went to my room, slammed the door, and collapsed on the bed. A few minutes passed and then there was a soft knock on the door.

"Mateo, can I come in?" Mom asked.

I really didn't want to talk. But maybe Mom

wouldn't stay long, or maybe she'd take one look at me and know I was at my breaking point. I stared at the wall and muttered, "Do whatever you want."

Mom slowly opened the door, looked around the room, then fixed her eyes on me.

"Are you having a rough day?"

I lied. "I'm fine, Mom."

"No, you're not. Talk to me. Maybe I can help?"

I didn't want to shut her out and be mean. Maybe talking would help.

"My day was the worst. Harris is spreading a rumor about me."

"Oh, Mateo, I'm so sorry. What did he say?"

"He told everyone Lily's my girlfriend, all because he saw us laughing together at lunch."

Mom looked relieved and confused. "Is that all? That's not so bad. She's such a nice girl."

"Geez, Mom, you don't understand. Lily's a friend, but she's not my girlfriend. It's embarrassing knowing everyone thinks we're together."

"Oh, I'm sorry. I didn't understand." Always the optimist, Mom searched for the silver lining.

"I bet most kids at school haven't even heard this rumor, or care. Maybe you're getting worked up over nothing?"

"I wish. A few guys already hassled me about it. They definitely believe Harris!"

"Have you talked to him? Tell him to knock it off. Maybe Harris doesn't realize how upset you are?"

"MOM! HE WON'T CARE. HE'S PROBABLY DOING IT ON PURPOSE, TO MAKE ME MAD."

"Well, he should care. He's supposed to be your friend. Friends shouldn't try to hurt or embarrass you."

Mom had a point. If I want this to stop, I need to go to the source directly. I told her I'd talk to Harris tomorrow. That made her happy. She gave me a big hug and said she's here for me whenever I need to talk. Dad too.

I DO FEEL BETTER NOW. TODAY WAS ROUGH BUT, HOPEFULLY, TALKING TO HARRIS WILL MAKE THINGS RIGHT.

CHAPTER THREE

Follow-Up Discussion Questions and Activities

Discussion Questions

1. Mateo was upset and wanted to be alone. When you're upset, how do you make yourself feel better?

   _____
   _____
   _____

   - Besides spending time alone, what else did Mateo do to deal with his feelings?

     _____
     _____
     _____

2. Mateo is upset about the rumor. Would you be upset if you were in his situation?

   _____
   _____
   _____

   - Why or why not?

     _____
     _____
     _____

3. Why do you think Mateo changed his mind and agreed to talk to his mom about what happened at school?

   _____
   _____
   _____

4. Mateo's mom didn't understand why he was upset. Have you ever been upset, and your parents didn't understand why? If so, in what types of situations does this usually happen?
_____
_____
_____

5. Why did Mateo feel better after talking to his mom?
_____
_____
_____

Activities

Writing Activity

1. Mateo feels embarrassed and upset about the rumor. What other feelings and thoughts might he have? From Mateo's perspective, write a journal entry describing his thoughts and feelings about Harris, the rumor, and his friends.

2. Mateo doesn't know why Harris started the rumor. Why do you think Harris started it, and how do you think he feels? From Harris's perspective, write a journal entry describing his thoughts and feelings about Mateo, Lily, and the rumor.

Self-Reflection Activity

1. Mateo's mom encourages him to talk things out with Harris to get him to stop spreading the rumor. Do you think this is a good strategy for Mateo? Explain why or why not.

Why Is He Spreading Rumors About Me?

Writing Activity Worksheet

From Mateo's perspective, write a journal entry describing his thoughts and feelings about Harris, the rumor, and his friends.

Journal ENTRY #1

Why Is He Spreading Rumors About Me?

Writing Activity Worksheet (continued)

From Harris's perspective, write a journal entry describing his thoughts and feelings about Mateo, Lily, and the rumor.

Journal ENTRY #2

_____
_____
_____
_____
_____
_____
_____
_____
_____
_____
_____
_____
_____
_____
_____
_____
_____
_____
_____
_____

Why Is He Spreading Rumors About Me?

Self-Reflection Activity Worksheet

Mateo's mom encourages him to talk things out with Harris to get him to stop spreading the rumor. Do you think this is a good strategy for Mateo? Explain why or why not.

_____
_____
_____
_____
_____
_____
_____
_____

TEACHER AND COUNSELOR ACTIVITY GUIDE

Chapter 4

I CAME TO SCHOOL HOPEFUL. HARRIS IS IN MY SECOND PERIOD SPANISH CLASS, SO I CAN TALK TO HIM THEN. MAYBE THIS WHOLE MESS CAN FINALLY BE OVER ONCE WE TALK IT OUT.

He was alone, sitting at his desk, when I saw him. It was now or never.

"Hola, Amigo," I said.

"Hey, Mateo. What's up?"

"Yesterday, some of the guys were asking me if Lily's my girlfriend because you told them she was."

"Hmmm. What'd you say?"

"Dude, come on. It's annoying that you keep telling people we're a couple. You KNOW we're not!"

"What do you mean I know? You guys might be keeping it secret."

"I'm telling you she's not my girlfriend. If you're my friend, you'll believe me."

"Fine. Whatever you say, Mateo."

"So you'll stop with all this stuff about me and Lily?"

"Hmmm... if it's not true, then why do you care so much?

"THAT'S WHY I CARE! CUZ IT'S NOT TRUE!"

Harris laughed in my face.

"Are you going to stop telling the whole school or not?"

"Mateo, if you're so freaked out, you tell everyone it's not true. I'm just sayin' what I saw."

Talking to him was pointless. I gave up and went back to my desk. I just hope he forgets about me and Lily, and then maybe everyone else will too.

Lunch was the first time I saw Lily since the rumor started. She was standing by the lunch counter and waved me over. Cupping her hands over her mouth, she softly asked if I'd heard the gossip going around school about us being boyfriend and girlfriend.

I nodded, leaned in, and whispered, "I tried to get Harris to stop. He's the one who started the rumor, but he just laughed at me."

"He's always starting drama. But I'm surprised he's spreading rumors about us. I thought you guys were friends?"

"Guess not," I said with a shrug.

"HEY, LOVEBIRDS!" The words ricocheted across the cafeteria. I recognized the voice immediately. It was Harris. Lily and I turned around and saw him with a big, smug grin on his face. He was giving Benjamin a fist bump, and the two of them were laughing and waiting for me at the table. When I sat down, I WAS SO ANGRY I DIDN'T EVEN LOOK AT HARRIS. I kept ignoring him. I don't even know why he sits with me and my friends. When lunch was over, I hurried out of the cafeteria with Tyler and Malik. I asked them why Harris is such a jerk sometimes, and if they had heard the lie he started about me and Lily.

"Yeah, I heard. But that's just Harris being Harris," Malik said.

"No one takes him seriously," added Tyler. "Just ignore him."

Chapter Four

Follow-Up Discussion Questions and Activities

Discussion Questions

1. The conversation between Mateo and Harris during Spanish class didn't go well. Whose fault was that and why?

   _____
   _____
   _____

2. Did Mateo do a good job speaking up for himself? Why or why not?

   _____
   _____
   _____

   - Should Mateo have said something different to Harris?

     _____
     _____
     _____

   - Was Mateo right to end the conversation when he did?

     _____
     _____
     _____

3. Do you think Harris and Mateo are friends? Why or why not?

   _____
   _____
   _____

4. Have you ever had a friend or acquaintance who acted like Harris?

5. Should Mateo and Lily have said or done something when Harris shouted "lovebirds" at them? Explain what they should have done differently.

6. Tyler and Malik are Mateo's best friends. Why do you think they didn't do more to help Mateo?

7. Do you think the kids sitting at Mateo's lunch table noticed he was upset?

- If so, do you think they knew who Mateo was angry at and why?

- Why do you think no one at the table tried to fix the situation?

- Tyler told Mateo to ignore Harris. Was that good advice? Why or why not?

TEACHER AND COUNSELOR ACTIVITY GUIDE

ACTIVITIES

Writing Activity

1. Mateo stopped talking to Harris once he realized it wasn't doing any good. What could he have said to Harris to convince him to stop spreading the rumor?

2. Write a new conversation between Mateo and Harris that ends with Harris apologizing and agreeing not to spread any more rumors.

3. Describe the setting (classroom, school hallway, playground, Mateo's home, etc.) where the conversation happens.

4. Have the conversation go back and forth. You can even have Harris deny starting the rumor, then admitting to it, and apologizing. Matteo should explain or give reasons why he wants the gossip and rumors to stop.

Group Work/Role-Play Activity

1. Ask students: Should Mateo's friends Tyler and Malik get involved in this situation? What should the two friends do to try to help resolve the situation between Mateo and Harris? How should they support Mateo?

2. Write their responses on the board so the students can see. (Responses can include the following: staying out of the situation; defending Mateo to Harris; telling Harris he can't sit at the lunch table if he keeps spreading rumors, etc.)

3. Have students choose the best response from Tyler and Malik.
   - Group students based on their choice.

4. Have each group create and perform a skit that demonstrates their chosen response, including the consequences it has for Tyler, Malik, Mateo, and Harris.

5. Lead a class discussion after each performance.
   - After all the skits are performed and discussed, ask students to vote on the response they think is the best one for Tyler and Malik.

Why Is He Spreading Rumors About Me?

Writing Activity Worksheet

Write a new conversation between Mateo and Harris that ends with Harris apologizing and agreeing not to spread any more rumors.

TEACHER AND COUNSELOR ACTIVITY GUIDE

Chapter 5

I LEFT SCHOOL ANGRY AND IN A BAD MOOD! AGAIN! I WENT STRAIGHT TO MY ROOM WHEN I GOT HOME. I WANTED TO BE ALONE, BUT MOM HAD OTHER IDEAS.

"Mateo, can I come in?" she asked. Her words had that "Mom tone," which meant she wasn't really asking, she was telling. A split second later she was in my room.

"Buddy, you look so sad. What happened? Is it the rumor again?"

"What do you think! I tried talking to Harris, like you said. He wouldn't listen. He laughed. He won't even admit to making up the rumor cuz he says it might be true."

"I'M SORRY, KIDDO. I THOUGHT MAYBE HE'D STOP IF HE KNEW HE WAS UPSETTING YOU. Did any of your friends say anything?"

"Not really. I asked Malik and Tyler if they thought Harris was being a jerk about it. They said no one takes him seriously and to just ignore him."

"Well, maybe they're right? If Harris can't get a rise out of you and Lily anymore, maybe he'll drop it."

"Maybe," I said, unconvinced.

"I know you're in a tough spot, Mateo. But please **TRY TO IGNORE THE RUMOR, OR AT LEAST PRETEND IT DOESN'T BOTHER YOU.** See if that changes things. If it doesn't, then maybe it's time to talk to a teacher or a counselor. I know you'll figure a way out of this. **THINGS WILL START TO GET BETTER!** I'll leave you alone now, but promise me you'll come down soon and play with your brothers and sister. They'll love it, and it'll take your mind off things. Plus, your dad and I need them occupied so we can finish making dinner!"

"Sure, I'll be down in a minute."

Over the next few days, I tried my best to do what Tyler, Malik, and Mom suggested – ignore the rumor. When anyone asked, I answered honestly and quickly. I said Lily's my friend, not my girlfriend. Then I changed the subject or walked away. Whenever Lily and I were together and someone called us out, we ignored them. But that didn't stop the rumor or the jokes.

AFTER A WHILE, TALKING TO LILY WAS JUST TOO HARD.

I was always distracted, thinking everyone who passed by would hassle us. Eventually, it got so awkward, we kept our interactions short and infrequent. Soon we stopped speaking altogether. Just the occasional wave hello.

It was really wild how quickly our relationship changed. Years of friendship trashed by a stupid rumor. I still like Lily, but it's too weird now. I can't listen to any more talk about her and me being together. I think she feels the same way. Maybe now the rumor will die since we're not hanging out. Of course, Harris still takes every opportunity to bring it up. The other day, when my buddies and I were making plans to play a game of hoops, Harris just had to throw another dig at me.

"Are you sure you can play, Mateo? Don't you need to check with Lily first?"

I stared him down. **"Give it a rest, Harris."**

This time, Tyler had my back. He told Harris to knock it off. I was glad one of my friends supported me. **I think my buddies finally got the clue that I was angry and didn't think any of it was funny.** They might even feel guilty for believing him and laughing along at the jokes. Maybe they want to make it up to me now?

I hope Harris gets the hint and stops running his mouth!

CHAPTER FIVE

Follow-Up Discussion Questions and Activities

Discussion Questions

1. Did you think if Mateo ignored the rumor, it would help?

   - Why or why not?

2. Have you ever been hurt by a rumor?

   - Share an example, if willing, but don't identify anyone by name.

3. When Mateo and Lily kept their distance from each other, did you think that would stop the rumor?

- Why or why not?

4. How do you think it made Mateo feel when he stopped hanging out with Lily?

5. Why do you think Tyler spoke up and supported Mateo in front of Harris?

6. How do you think Mateo felt when Tyler defended him?

Activities

Art Activity

1. Remind students how Mateo's mom encouraged him to play with his siblings to get his mind off his problem. What activities help you relax and make you forget your troubles?

2. Draw a picture of yourself doing an activity that relaxes you or helps you cope with stress. Write down the feelings and thoughts you experience when doing this activity. Are you able to forget about your problems or not?

Group Activity

1. Ask students: Why didn't Tyler and Malik speak up or defend their friend Mateo?

2. Write the responses on the board. (Answers can include the following: they thought Mateo wasn't upset by the rumors; they believed Mateo thought the rumor was funny; they believed the rumor; no one wanted to make Harris angry, etc.)

3. Ask students to choose which is the most likely reason Tyler and Malik didn't speak up, then group students based on their choice.

4. Have each group brainstorm different responses or actions Malik and Tyler could have taken right away to help resolve the situation.

5. Ask each group to share one of the responses or actions they came up with. Then, as a class, discuss its pros and cons.

6. After all groups have shared with the class, have students vote on which action they think will be most successful to stop the rumor and help everyone get along.

TEACHER AND COUNSELOR ACTIVITY GUIDE 47

Why Is He Spreading Rumors About Me?

Art Activity Worksheet

Draw a picture of yourself doing an activity that relaxes you or helps you cope with stress.

Why Is He Spreading Rumors About Me?

Art Activity Worksheet Continued

Write down the feelings and thoughts you experience when doing this activity. Are you able to forget about your problems or not?

Thoughts and Feelings:
_____
_____
_____
_____
_____
_____
_____
_____

TEACHER AND COUNSELOR ACTIVITY GUIDE

Chapter 6

Usually I walk home from school, but not today. Mom's picking me up. That means standing outside and waiting in the vehicle pick-up line. As I stood there, I thought about how sad and frustrated I've felt since Harris started the rumor. I still can't believe how that rumor completely torched my friendship with Lily. And it blows me away that Harris didn't stop spreading the rumor, especially since I asked him to. I thought he was a better friend than that. He doesn't respect my feelings, which tells me he's not a good friend.

When I looked up to see who else was standing in the pick-up line, I saw Lily. I had forgotten how much she HATES riding the bus. Every day, her parents shuttle her to and from school. When she looked in my direction, I gave her a big wave and walked right up to her.

"HEY! WHAT'S UP?" I asked.

Lily glanced over her shoulders, as if to make sure no one was watching us.

"How've you been?" she whispered. "Haven't heard from you in a while."

I nodded knowingly. I felt bad about not talking to her for so long, and I felt even worse seeing how uncomfortable she was talking to me now.

"It's been so weird ever since that rumor started," I admitted.

Lily kept glancing around, never really looking at me.

"I know," she said. "I was afraid if I talked to you, the rumor would blow up even more."

"I get it. Hanging out got to be a drag. It wasn't fun, not like it used to be."

"Totally! Everyone staring. Asking questions about us. Making stuff up. But I didn't think we'd stop being friends, Mateo."

"Me either. I hate this. We've always been good, Lily. Why should we let Harris's lie change that?"

Lily finally stopped looking around and faced me. Out loud, she said exactly what I was thinking:

"I MISS BEING FRIENDS."

"ME TOO," I said.

In the corner of my eye, I saw Mom pull up to the

curb. It was time to go. I told Lily it was good to finally talk. She smiled and said she'd see me tomorrow. That made me happy. I had my friend back. Even though I have lots of good buddies, I was lonely without her friendship.

"So you and Lily are talking again, huh?" Mom asked as we pulled away from school.

"Yeah, it's all good."

"THAT'S GREAT, MATEO! BUT WHAT ABOUT THE RUMOR YOU WERE SO WORRIED ABOUT? HAS IT FINALLY BLOWN OVER?"

"NOT REALLY. BUT WE DECIDED TO HANG OUT ANYWAY."

"I'm so happy to hear that! You shouldn't lose a friend because of a rumor, especially when neither of you did anything wrong. Harris and everyone else will figure out you're just friends, and the rumor will be forgotten. But if it does keep going around school, I think you should talk to your teacher or the school counselor and ask their advice. Or, if you want, I can call and talk to someone at school for you."

"Umm… you don't need to do that, Mom. It's all good."

The next day, I had math class with Lily. She was happy to see me and asked if I'd finished the assignment.

"Most of it," I confessed.

She giggled. "Mateo, you're SOOO lucky Mr. Ramirez doesn't grade our homework."

"I know, but I understand it at least." We laughed. It felt just like old times.

"OOOOHHHH! YOU TWO STILL CRUSHIN ON EACH OTHER, AND IN MATH CLASS. HA!" blabbed Harris.

We looked at him. I froze, not knowing what to say. But Lily gave it to him good.

"OH PLEASE, HARRIS! WE'RE FRIENDS, NOT A COUPLE, AND YOU KNOW IT! GO GET A NEW HOBBY THAT DOESN'T INVOLVE SPREADING RUMORS. NO ONE'S LISTENING TO YOUR LIES ANYMORE."

Harris rolled his eyes. He mumbled "whatever" and slunk back to his desk. He pretty much left us alone after that. He stopped spreading rumors and talking trash. I think he knew he couldn't get the reaction he wanted anymore.

Before all this happened, I never thought one rumor could make such a mess of things or cause so much trouble. But it did. A rumor almost wrecked me and Lily. I'M GLAD WE STOOD UP TO HARRIS AND STOOD UP FOR WHAT WE WANTED! A GREAT FRIENDSHIP!

CHAPTER SIX

Follow-Up Discussion Questions and Activities

Discussion Questions

1. Why do you think Mateo talked to Lily in the school pick-up line?

2. What do you think made Mateo more nervous: Talking to Lily? Being seen with Lily? Hearing and seeing Lily's reaction to him?

   - Explain your answer.

3. Why do you think Lily was kind to Mateo, even though she seemed tentative?

4. When Harris hassled Mateo and Lily in math class, how do you think it made Mateo feel?

- What emotions do you think Lily felt?

   _____
   _____
   _____

5. Did it surprise you that Lily, not Mateo, responded to Harris in math class? Explain.

   _____
   _____
   _____

6. Why do you think Harris stopped spreading the rumor and bothering Mateo and Lily?

   _____
   _____
   _____

Activities

Self-Reflection Activity

1. Explain to students: Mateo and Lily tried several strategies to get Harris to stop spreading the rumor.

    - What other strategies could they have tried?
    - What strategy would you have used and why?
    - Write a short story or draw a comic strip in which Mateo and Lily use your strategy to confront Harris and stop the rumor.

Group Activity/Role-Play Activity

1. Divide students into groups of three or four.
2. Have each group write a different ending to the story and tell them to be prepared to act out their new ending for the class. (Endings can include the following: Mateo and Lily stop being friends; More rumors spread, and Lily gets mad at Mateo; Mateo drifts away from all his friends; Mateo spreads a rumor about Harris, etc.)
3. After each group performs their skit, discuss the consequences rumors can have on individuals (low self-esteem, loss of confidence, anxiety, depression, more absences from school, etc.).

Why Is He Spreading Rumors About Me?

Self-Reflection Activity Worksheet

Write a short story or draw a comic strip that explains the strategy you think Mateo and Lily should have used to stop the rumor.

Short Story:

_____
_____
_____
_____

Comic Strip:

Why Is He Spreading Rumors About Me?

GROUP ACTIVITY/ROLE-PLAY ACTIVITY WORKSHEET

Write a diffrent ending to the story.

_____
_____
_____
_____
_____
_____

Boys Town Press Books
Kid-friendly books for teaching social skills

A book series and accompanying activity guides focused on changing friendships, finding your place, advocating for yourself, and being true to who you are.

978-1-944882-63-1
978-1-944882-64-8

978-1-944882-65-5
978-1-944882-66-2

978-1-944882-67-9
978-1-944882-68-6

978-0-938510-68-0
978-0-938510-69-7

Navigating Friendships
Jennifer Licate
GRADES 4-7

978-1-944882-94-5
978-1-944882-95-2

978-1-9444882-89-1
978-1-944882-90-7

A book series teaching important lessons about lying, cheating, and being a good friend.

978-1-934490-94-5

978-1-944882-03-7

978-1-944882-10-5

978-1-944882-21-1

978-1-944882-32-7

For information on Boys Town and its Education Model, Common Sense Parenting®, and training programs:
LiftwithBoysTown.org | Parenting.org
training@boystown.org | 800-545-5771

For parenting and educational books and other resources:
BoysTownPress.org
btpress@boystown.org | 800-282-6657